MAMA DON'T ALLOW

Miles got a saxophone for his birthday.

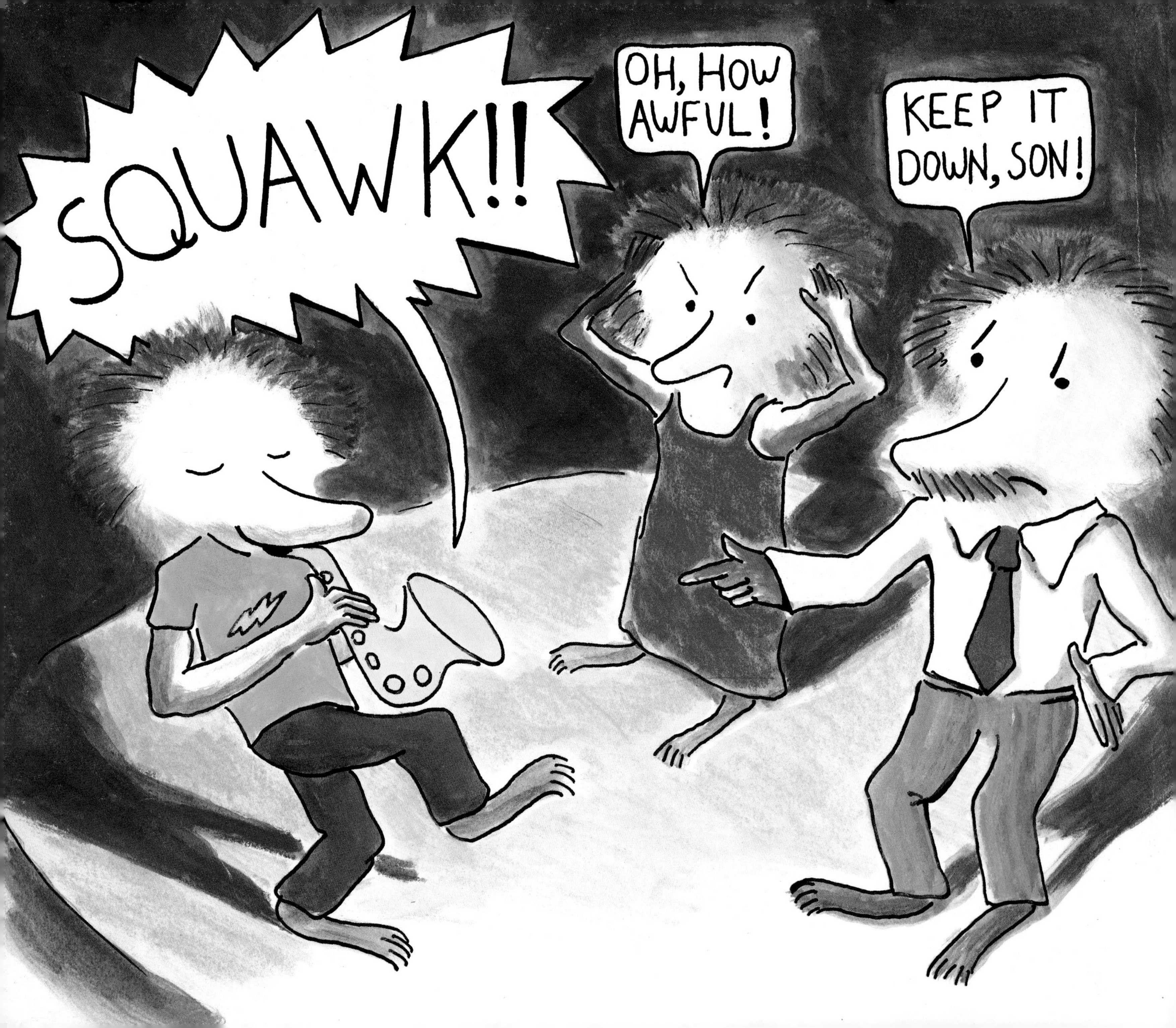
SQUAWK!!
OH, HOW AWFUL!
KEEP IT DOWN, SON!

Miles practiced,

and practiced, until his mama and papa
couldn't stand it anymore,
and his mama said:

And so he did,
as loud as could be.

Miles strolled down Main Street,
where he met a drummer named Al;

up Swamp Lane,
where he met a guitarist
named Bert;

and over Bayou Bridge,
where he met a trumpet player
named Doc.

"Hey, let's play some music!" said Miles.

"Loud music!" said Al.

"Let's be a band!" said Bert.

"The Swamp Band!" cried Doc.

And they played as loud as they could.

Soon the whole town cried out:

But down in the swamp
at the edge of town

the sharp-toothed,
long-tailed,
yellow-eyed alligators said:

Saturday night when the sun went down,
the alligators came from miles around.
They were dressed in their finest.

The Swamp Band played their favorite song.

The Swamp Band played far into the night.

When the music was over
the band was hungry.
So were the alligators.

The alligators snapped their jaws
and smacked their lips.

And so the band sang...

A Lullaby of Swampland:

The alligators fell fast asleep.
Miles piloted the riverboat
back to Swampville.
The Swamp Band tiptoed home,

And Mama said:

MAMA DON'T ALLOW

Traditional
arr. by Mark Shafarman

Lively
E7   A

Well now, Ma - ma don't allow no mu - sic play - in' 'round here, Ma - ma don't allow no

E7   A7   D7

mu - sic play - in' 'round here, Now we don't care what Ma - ma don't allow gon - na play that mu - sic

Dm7   A   E7   A   E7

a - ny how, Ma - ma don't allow no mu - sic play - in' 'round here. Well now,

Mama don't allow no guitar playin' 'round here,
Mama don't allow no guitar playin' 'round here,
Now we don't care what Mama don't allow,
Gonna play that music anyhow,
Mama don't allow no guitar playin' 'round here.
Well now,

Mama don't allow no piano playin' 'round here,
Mama don't allow no piano playin' 'round here,
Now we don't care what Mama don't allow,
Gonna play that music anyhow,
Mama don't allow no piano playin' 'round here.
Well now,

Make up your own verses as you sing this song:
"Mama don't allow no foot stompin'," etc., etc.

Copyright © 1984 by Thacher Hurd
Printed in Hong Kong.   All rights reserved.

Library of Congress Cataloging-in-Publication Data
Hurd, Thacher. Mama don't allow.

*   Summary: Miles and the Swamp Band have the time of*
their lives playing at the Alligator Ball, until they
discover the menu includes Swamp Band Soup.
*   [1. Bands (Music)—Fiction.   2. Musicians—Fiction.*
3. Alligators—Fiction.   4. Swamps—Fiction]   I. Title.
PZ7.H9562Mam 1984   [E]   83-47703
ISBN 0-06-022689-7   ISBN 0-06-022690-0 (lib. bdg.)
ISBN 0-06-443078-2 (pbk.)

First Harper Trophy Edition, 1985